Sara Swan Miller

TURKEYS
ON THE
TRAIN

TURKEYS ON THE TRAIN

iUniverse books may be ordered through booksellers or by contacting:

iUniverse
1663 Liberty Drive
Bloomington, IN 47403
www.iuniverse.com
844-349-9409

Because of the dynamic nature of the Internet, any web addresses or links contained in this book may have changed since publication and may no longer be valid. The views expressed in this work are solely those of the author and do not necessarily reflect the views of the publisher, and the publisher hereby disclaims any responsibility for them.

Any people depicted in stock imagery provided by Getty Images are models, and such images are being used for illustrative purposes only. Certain stock imagery © Getty Images.

ISBN: 978-1-6632-0980-1 (sc)
ISBN: 978-1-6632-0996-2 (hc)
ISBN: 978-1-6632-0981-8 (e)

Library of Congress Control Number: 2020918704

Print information available on the last page.

iUniverse rev. date: 10/01/2020

TO JIM, JUDY, AND HENRY,

for all of the lovely Thanksgiving celebrations

It was a beautiful fall day in the woods. The little turkey flock was having a fine time scratching around in the fallen leaves and finding tasty treats underneath.

"Putt, putt!" said Veronica. "A snail! Yum!
"Putt, putt, PUTT!" said Ramona.
"Another one! Awfully crunchy, though."

"Putt, putt, putt! OOH!" cried Grace. "Look at these crabapples!"

Putt! Come over here, girls," called Esmerelda.

Putt! Putt! Hundreds and hundreds of acorns all over the ground! Dig in! Putt, putt, putt, putt, PUTT!"

Everyone ran over to the acorn treasure trove. Esmerelda was the leader. The others always did what she told them to because she knew best.

Scratch, scratch, scratch! Putt, putt, putt! They all got to work gobbling up the acorns.
"Delicious!" they all agreed. "This is the life!" Then they heard something coming.

"Oh, trouble, trouble trouble!" it called. "Trouble, trouble, trouble, trouble!"

"What ever is that?" asked Grace.

"I don't know," said Esmerelda. "But it sounds like, well, trouble!"

Then a big farm turkey came running and waddling crazily through the trees. She ran right up to Veronica, Ramona, Grace, and Esmerelda.

"Help! Help! They want to eat poor Tilly! Me! Tilly!" she cried. "Oh, trouble, trouble, trouble!"

"Heavens!" said Esmerelda. "Calm down. Who wants to eat you?"

"The farmers! But I got away! Oh, trouble, trouble, trouble."

"It's all right," said Esmerelda. "You're safe now, here with us!"

"There, there, Tilly," said Grace.

"You can live with us," said Ramona. "There's plenty of food."

"No one will find you here!" said Veronica.

But just then, the turkeys heard, off in the woods, the sound of men yelling!

"Where is that silly bird?" yelled one.

"This way!" yelled another. "I can see her tracks!"

"Oh, no!" cried Esmerelda. "Fly away! Fly, fly!"

"But I can't fly!" cried Tilly. "Oh, trouble, trouble, trouble, trouble."

"Then run!" cried Esmeralda. "Come on! Run! Run!"

Off they all ran as fast as they could go. For Tilly, that wasn't very fast.

"Can't you run any faster?" asked Esmerelda?

"No!" panted Tilly.

"Well, try! Faster, faster!" cried Esmeralda. "Let's make tracks!"

Suddenly she stopped short. The other turkeys nearly ran her over.

"I know! That's it!" she cried. "We'll hop a train! Come on! This way!"

Esmerelda led them on over hill and dale, all the way to the train station. They clustered together on the platform.

"Where's the train?" said Veronica.

"Come on, train. Come on train!" said Ramona.

And here it came! With a horrible shrieking, it came roaring into the station. Scary!

"Never mind the racket!" cried Esmerelda. "Hop on, girls!"

They all hopped on—except Tilly. She tried, but her legs were too short.

"Help!" she cried. "Oh, trouble, trouble, trouble."

The other turkeys hopped back down.

"Okay!" cried Esmerelda. "One, two, three, boost!"

With a great heave, they pushed Tilly onto the train. She landed on her beak, but she was all right.

"Quick! Hide!" cried Esmerelda.

They all dived under the seats and held their breath. With a great LURCH the train began to move. Faster and faster. Pocketa, pocketa, pocketa!

"Whew!" whispered Esmerelda. "Safe!"

For a while, they rocked along with the train. Finally, Esmerelda stuck her head out. None of the people on the train noticed. Some were talking into little boxes. Some were scratching at bigger boxes on their laps. Others were bouncing up and down with wires coming out of their ears.

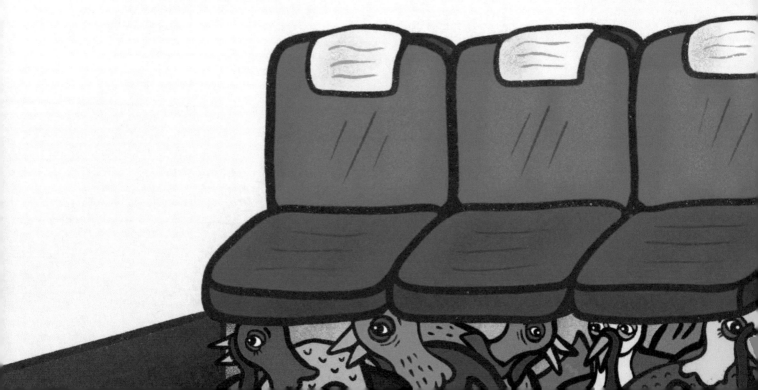

"Putt, putt!" said Esmerelda.
"No one even sees we're here!"
She looked around some more.
She spotted some little white bits
on the floor.
"Come on out, girls!" she said.
"I found food!"

Very carefully the turkeys stuck their heads out. Very, very carefully they crept out and looked around. It was true! Nobody was paying any attention to them.

They pounced on the little bits and began gobbling them up. It was a fine feast.

Just then, the train slowed and pulled to a stop.

"RIDGEWOOD!"

boomed a voice.

Some of the people started to get up.

"Hide, girls!" cried Esmerelda.

They all dived back under the seats.

"ALL ABOARD!"

boomed the voice.

Then, LURCH! The train started up again. Pocketa, pocketa, pocketa. The turkeys peeked out again. Still no one seemed to see them.

They all went back to work on the little tasty bits.

"People surely do leave a mess," said Grace.

"Good thing!" said Tilly.

The turkeys were having a fine time, except when the train came to another station. They all hid under the seats until it started up again.

Gobble gobble, dive! Gobble gobble, dive!
The turkeys thought no one noticed them at all,
but that wasn't quite true. Tucked into a corner seat,
a woman named Marge was watching everything
they did. She was smiling and clutching her
binoculars. Marge figured out what must have
happened. She wondered what the turkeys would do

“LAST STOP! SUFFERN!

Everybody off the train!” boomed the big voice.

"Suffern?!" screeched Tilly. "We're in SUFFERN?!
I have enough suffern! Oh, trouble, trouble, trouble,
trouble."

"This is terrible!" shrieked Veronica.

"Horrible!" cried Grace.

"A disaster!" screamed Ramona.

"Oh, dear, dear, dear!" said Esmerelda. "Anyhow,
girls, this is where we get out."

They all tumbled off the train and milled around
on the platform.

"What are we going to DO?" said Tilly. "We can't
stay here in SUFFERN!"

Now, now, everybody," said Esmerelda. "Calm down. I'll think of something."

But she couldn't. She thought and thought. Then she thought some more. She was thinking so hard that she didn't notice Marge until she was right in front of them.

"You poor turkeys!" said Marge. "Can I help you? You seem to be in trouble."

"Eeek! Trouble, trouble, trouble, trouble!" shrieked Tilly. "Suffern! Suffern!"

"What's wrong, dears?" asked Marge. "Oh, let me see if I can guess. You don't like it here in Suffern."

"Trouble, trouble, trouble!" cried Tilly, nodding her head up and down.

Esmerelda didn't know whether to trust this woman or run away. It's hard to be the one in charge. She decided to trust.

"Well, how would you like to go home with me?" said Marge. I live in Paradise. Paradise, Pennsylvania, that is."

"PARADISE?"

Esmerelda almost fell over. Veronica, Ramona, Grace, and Tilly did! Marge helped them back on their feet.

"Do you all want to come to Paradise?" asked Marge. "My car is right over there."

The turkeys all looked at each other.

"Let's do it!" said Esmerelda.

Marge led them, tumbling all over each other, to a small car a few steps away. It was a very, very small car, but they managed to wedge themselves in somehow.

Tilly got to sit in the front seat because she was so large. And off they went.

"Putt, putt, putt, putt," said the car.

"Hey, the car talks turkey!" said Ramona.

"Paradise! Here we come!" cried Esmerelda.

The End.

About The Author

Sara Swan Miller is the author of more than 70 books for children. Her works about animals show an uncanny ability to speak the minds and zany imaginations of cats, dogs, and other critters. Her memories of a wonderfully playful childhood are carried into the way she captures the language of children of any age.

And so, children as well as their parents love the authenticity of Sara's writing. They show the skill and warmth that guided her careers as a Montessori teacher, an outdoor environmental educator, and a parent. Sara's books that ask children to read dedicated stories to their pet dog, cat, or where a live animal isn't around, their teddy bear, have not only encouraged new readers to bring their pets to school (when allowed), but have had bigger effects: less TV, more reading for the fun of it. You can find those books at online sources, or ask at your favorite local bookstore.

Sara passed away in 2020. But the legacy of her stories will delight children as well as their parents for all the years to come.

About The Illustrator

Abby Liscum is a graphic designer from upstate New York. She graduated from the Tyler School of Art and Architecture in Philadelphia with a focus in illustration and animation. She was awarded the Allen Koss Senior Portfolio Award in Graphic & Interactive Design for Motion. Her past work includes creating graphics for several grassroots activist organizations and she enjoys experimenting with different forms of design.

Printed in the United States
By Bookmasters